Words to Know Before You Read

Let's Learn The
Dd Sound

dad	do
Dave	doctor
deep	does
dig	dogs
dinosaur	door
dirt	duck
dish	

www.rourkeeducationalmedia.com

Edited by Luana Mitten
Illustrated by Mike Byrne
Art Direction, Cover and Page Layout by Tara Raymo

Library of Congress PCN Data

The Duck Doctor / Precious McKenzie
ISBN 978-1-62169-260-7 (hard cover) (alk. paper)
ISBN 978-1-62169-218-8 (soft cover)
Library of Congress Control Number: 2012952756

Rourke Educational Media
Printed in the United States of America,
North Mankato, Minnesota

rourkeeducationalmedia.com

customerservice@rourkeeducationalmedia.com • PO Box 643328 Vero Beach, Florida 32964

The Duck Doctor

Counselor
Freya

Doctor
Sue

Levi

Yolie

Tucker

Written By Precious McKenzie
Illustrated By Mike Byrne

"Let's meet an animal doctor," says Counselor Freya.

"Does she help big or small animals?" asks Levi.

"All shapes and sizes," says Counselor Freya.

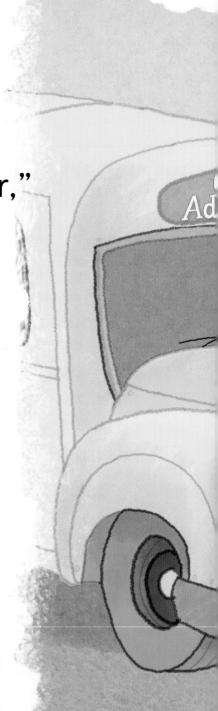

"Look at all of the dogs in the waiting room!" shouts Tucker.

"They do not look happy," remarks Levi.

"Hello, I am Doctor Sue," says a woman in a white coat.

The children hear a strange sound coming from behind the door.

"Someone sounds sick," says Levi.

"Sounds like a dinosaur to me," whispers Tucker.

9

"Let's take a look at my new patient," says Doctor Sue.

"This little duck lost his mom and dad," the doctor tells them.

"What should we do?" asks Yolie.

"Give the duck a dish of water to drink," says Doctor Sue.

Doctor Sue listens to his heartbeat. She checks his temperature. She gives the duck medicine.

"Now to find this little duck a new home," says Doctor Sue.

"Can we take the duck back to the camp?" Counselor Freya asks.

"Yes, he would like the trees and fresh air at camp," Levi adds.

Doctor Sue thinks and thinks. Then she says, "Yes!"

15

The children work together to build a pen for the little duck. They put a dish for food and a dish for water in the pen.

They dig a deep hole in the dirt. They fill the hole with water.

"His swimming pool is ready!" yells Yolie.

Their little duck splishes and splashes in his pool. He loves his new home. The children love him too.

Levi yells, "Let's name him Dave!"

After Reading Word Study

Picture Glossary

Directions: Look at each picture and read the definition. Write a list of all of the words you know that start with the same sound as *Dave*. Remember to look in the book for more words.

dig (DIG): When you dig you use a shovel to move soil.

dirt (DURT): Dirt is another name for soil, or earth.

dish (DISH): A dish is a container, like a bowl or plate, that holds food or water.

doctor (DOK-tur): A doctor is someone who has gone to medical school and knows how to take care of sick people or animals.

dogs (DAWGZ): Dogs are furry, four legged animals that bark. People like to keep dogs as pets.

duck (DUHK): A duck is a bird that has a bill, webbed feet, and swims in the water.

About the Author

Precious McKenzie lives in Montana with her husband and three children. She loves ducks of all shapes and sizes. But she has never had a duck for a pet. She has a parrot.

Ask The Author!
www.rem4students.com

About the Illustrator

Mike Byrne grew up near Liverpool, but moved to London to work as an illustrator by day and a crayon wielding crime fighter by night. He now lives in the countryside with his Wifey and two cats, where he spends his days doodling and making children's books fueled only by cups of tea & cookies.

Comprehension & Word Study:

- Retell the Story:

  What happened first?

  What happened next?

  How does the story end?

  What was the most exciting part for you?

- Word Study: Building Words

  Read each of the sound words from the book with your students and write them on the board. Have your students use letter tiles to build each word as you read it. Ask students to think of a sentence using each sound word. Have them orally share the sentence with the class.

Sound Words I Used:

dad
Dave
deep
dig
dinosaur
dirt
dish
do
doctor
does
dogs
door
duck

Let's Learn The **Dd** Sound

The Duck Doctor

Sound Adventures

Sound Adventures is a fresh approach to traditional phonics based readers. With delightful stories, they build vocabulary and encourage readers to apply what they are learning about letters and sounds. Come along on wild journeys with the characters from Camp Adventure!

ISBN 978-1-6216-9218-8

90000

9 781621 692188

by

Rourke
Educational Media
rourkeeducationalmedia.com

SLEDDING in SUMMER?

SLEDDING SLOPE

CAMP ADVENTURE

Ss
Blends
Sound
Adventures

Teaching Focus:

Beginning Blends

Blends are two or three consonants that hook the sounds together. Write the words sled, snow, stop, and small on the board. Circle the blends so students have a better understanding of what a blend is and looks like. Read each word aloud and have your students echo you.

Teacher Notes available at
rem4teachers.com

Tips for Reading this Book with Children:

1. Read the title and make predictions about the story.

Predictions – after reading the title have students make predictions about the book.

2. Take a picture walk.

Talk about the pictures in the book. Implant the vocabulary as you take the picture walk.

Have children find one or two words they know as they do a picture walk.

3. Have students look at the first pages of the book and find a word that begins with the letter or sound focus of the book.

4. Ask students to think of other words that begin with that same sound.

5. Strategy Talk – use to assist students while reading.
- Get your mouth ready
- Look at the picture
- Think…does it make sense
- Think…does it look right
- Think…does it sound right
- Chunk it – by looking for a part you know

6. Read it again.

7. Complete the activities at the end of the book.